TELL ME MORE! science
ICEBERGS

by Ruth Owen

Prospect Heights Public Library
12 N Elm Street
Prospect Heights, IL 60070
www.phpl.info

Ruby Tuesday Books

Published in 2021 by Ruby Tuesday Books Ltd.

Copyright © 2021 Ruby Tuesday Books Ltd.
All rights reserved. No part of this publication may be reproduced in whole or in part, stored in any retrieval system, or transmitted in any form or by any means, electronic, mechanical, photocopying, recording, or otherwise, without written permission from the publisher.

Designer: Emma Randall
Editor: Mark J. Sachner
Production: John Lingham

Photo credits:
Alamy: 19; FLPA: 5, 8; NASA: 4, 11; Nature Picture Library: 14–15, 16–17, 18, 20 (top), 21; Shutterstock: Cover, 1, 6–7, 9, 10–11, 12–13, 17 (top), 20 (bottom), 21 (top), 22–23.

Library of Congress Control Number: 2020946814
Print (hardback) ISBN 978-1-78856-168-6
Print (paperback) ISBN 978-1-78856-169-3
eBook ISBN 978-1-78856-170-9

Printed and published in the United States of America
For further information including rights and permissions requests, please contact: **shan@rubytuesdaybooks.com**

Contents

What Is an Iceberg? 4

How Do Icebergs Form? 6

Crack! A New Iceberg 8

The Biggest-Ever Iceberg 10

The Tip of an Iceberg 12

Iceberg Shapes 14

Blue and Striped Icebergs 16

Upside-Down or Trapped! 18

Icebergs Help Animals 20

Be an Iceberg Scientist 22

Glossary, How Do Scientists Name Icebergs? 23

Index, Read More, Answers 24

What Is an Iceberg?

Icebergs are giant chunks of ice that float in the ocean.

They are made from frozen **freshwater**, not seawater.

An iceberg may be as tall as a 25-story building!

Icebergs are mostly found in icy oceans in the Arctic and around Antarctica.

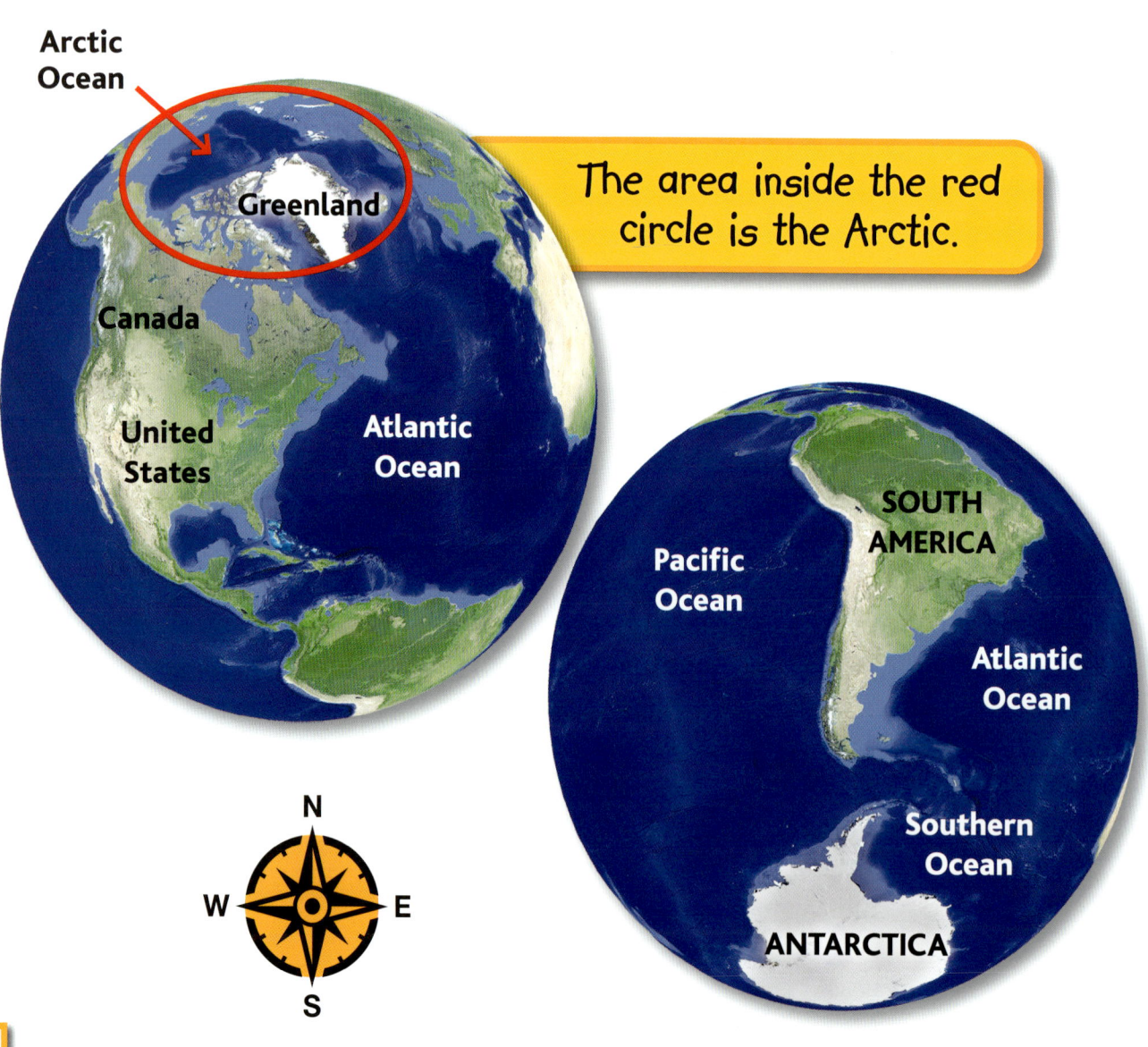

The area inside the red circle is the Arctic.

An iceberg that is less than 16 feet (5 m) tall is called a "bergy bit." A small iceberg that's about the size of a van is called a "growler."

An iceberg in Greenland

How Do Icebergs Form?

Icebergs come from thick sheets of ice called **glaciers** and **ice shelves**.

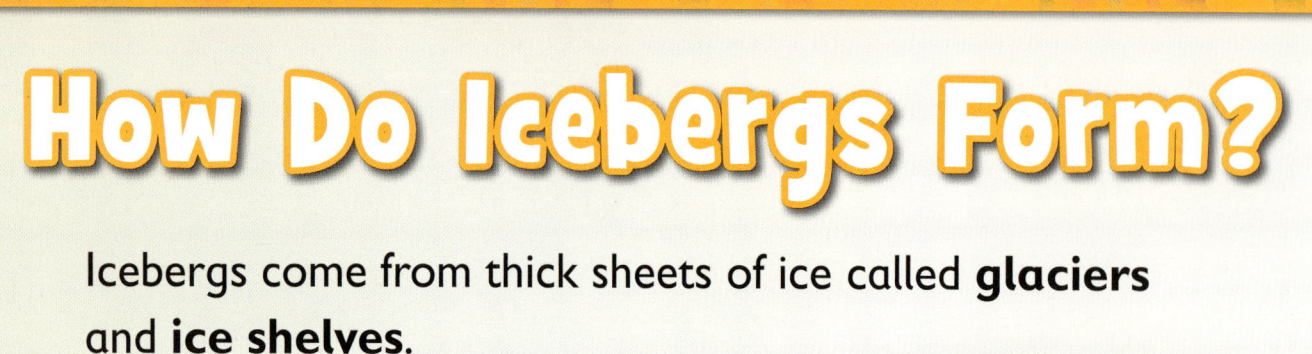

Glacier

Mountains

Ocean

6

A glacier forms when snow falls in a **valley** between mountains.

It is too cold for the snow to melt, so it turns to ice.

Year after year, more snow falls and becomes ice.

The thick sheet of ice is called a glacier.

It can take thousands of years for a glacier to form. The ice in some very deep glaciers in Antarctica may be up to 1 million years old!

Crack! A New Iceberg

Icebergs forming

Face of a glacier

A glacier is so heavy that it slowly slides downhill, like a river of ice.

Eventually some glaciers reach the ocean.

Then chunks of the glacier break off into the water and become icebergs.

Sometimes the front, or face, of a glacier keeps on slowly moving out into the sea.

Then it forms a thick sheet of floating ice called an **ice shelf**.

Ice shelf

If the ice shelf cracks, the pieces become icebergs.

When a chunk of ice breaks away from a glacier or ice shelf, it is called **calving**.

Let's Talk

Sometimes, small icebergs form out at sea. How?

(The answer is on page 24.)

The Biggest-Ever Iceberg

In 2000, a huge iceberg broke away from an ice shelf in Antarctica.

It was the size of Connecticut—the biggest iceberg that scientists had ever tracked!

They named it iceberg B-15.

B-15 floated around Antarctica, but then began to break into pieces.

This piece of B-15 was 32 miles (51 km) long.

The pieces traveled for thousands of miles before they melted.

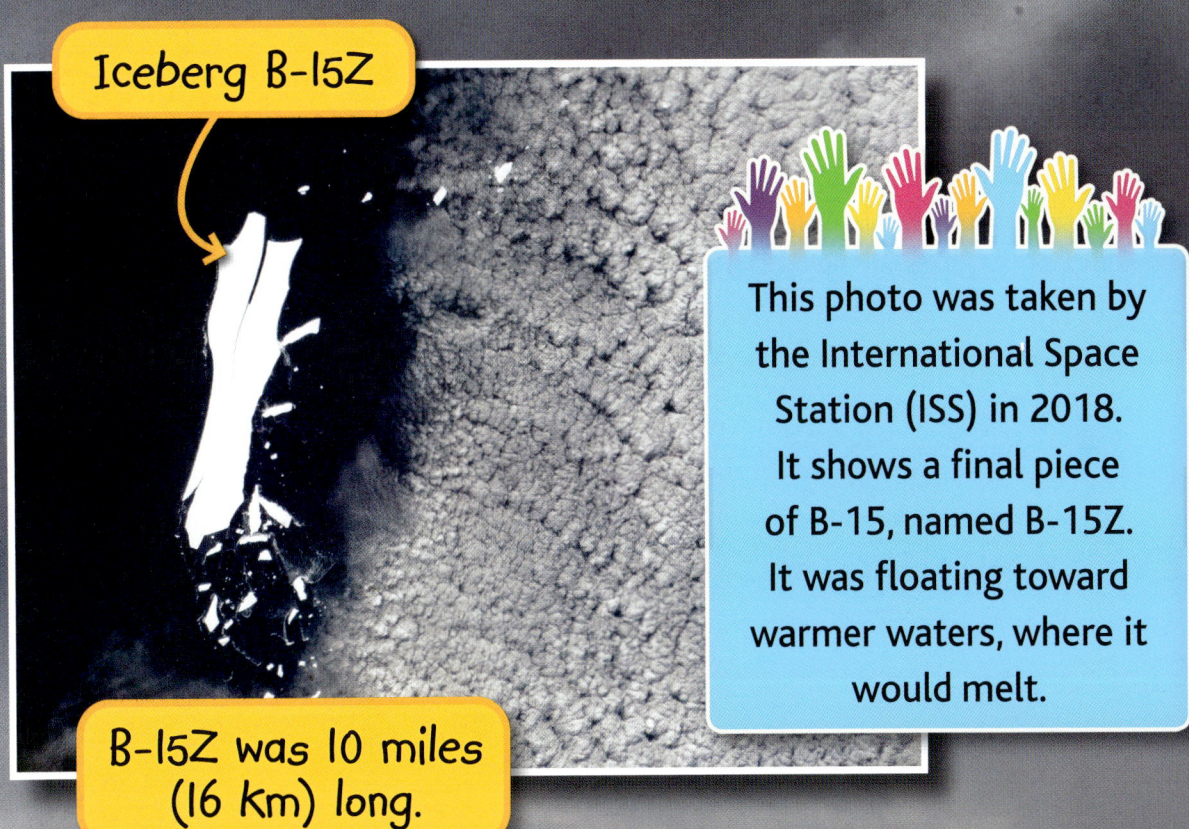

Iceberg B-15Z

B-15Z was 10 miles (16 km) long.

This photo was taken by the International Space Station (ISS) in 2018. It shows a final piece of B-15, named B-15Z. It was floating toward warmer waters, where it would melt.

Discover how scientists name icebergs on page 23.

Psst . . . Turn your book clockwise.

The Tip of an Iceberg

Just like an ice cube in a glass of soda, an iceberg floats in water.

However, not all of an iceberg can be seen on the surface.

In fact, about 90 percent of an iceberg is floating under the water!

12

Have you ever heard someone say "it's just the tip of the iceberg"? It means that what you can see is just a small part of what's going on. The saying comes from the fact that we can only see the top, or tip, of an iceberg.

This illustration shows how an iceberg might look underwater.

Iceberg Shapes

Icebergs are shaped by the air and water around them.

If an iceberg floats into a warmer area, the warm air and water start to melt it.

Waves crash against icebergs, making them crack and break apart.

Sometimes an iceberg changes shape when it crashes into rocks or another iceberg!

Tabular iceberg

A tabular iceberg has steep sides and a flat top like a table.

Spire

Some icebergs have spires, like a church.

Some of this iceberg has melted at the surface.

Iceberg underwater

Let's Talk

What do you think made the shapes on this iceberg?

(The answer is on page 24.)

Blue and Striped Icebergs

An iceberg is covered with ice that's made of tightly packed snow.

The snow contains lots of air bubbles that make it look white.

Stripes

Sometimes, as a glacier slides downhill, soil from the ground mixes with the ice. The soil forms layers in the ice that get trapped in the glacier. When an iceberg calves from the glacier, the soil layers look like stripes.

Sometimes an iceberg or part of an iceberg looks blue.

That's because it's made of ice that contains hardly any air.

Blue ice

Let's Talk

How would you describe the shape of this iceberg?

Upside-Down or Trapped!

As an iceberg melts or gets battered by waves, its shape and weight changes.

The iceberg may get too heavy on one side.

A large piece of underwater ice may break off.

Then whoosh! Suddenly the iceberg flips upside-down.

The iceberg in the photo has flipped. The jagged, blue ice was once the bottom of the iceberg under the water.

Sometimes the ocean around an iceberg freezes.

Then the iceberg is trapped until the water **thaws**.

A trapped iceberg

Frozen ocean

Icebergs Help Animals

The bald rockcod fish lives in and around icebergs.

Its body contains special substances that keep its blood from freezing.

Bald rockcod

As an iceberg melts, **particles** of soil that were trapped in the ice get into the water. The particles contain **nutrients**. Tiny, plant-like **phytoplankton** in the ocean feed on these nutrients.

Phytoplankton seen under a microscope.

20

Chinstrap penguins hunt for fish and shrimp in freezing Antarctic seas.

They swim up to 50 miles (80 km) from the shore to find food.

They jump up onto icebergs to rest and stay safe from hungry leopard seals.

Chinstrap penguin

Be an Iceberg Scientist

An iceberg may be as big as a small town. But you can make little icebergs in your freezer and discover how they float and change shape.

Gather Your Equipment:

- 2 small plastic bags (with rubber bands if needed)
- Measuring cup
- Water
- Scissors
- A large bowl (see-through if possible)
- A notebook and pen
- A ruler
- An adult helper
- A timer

1 Carefully pour half a pint (0.2 l) of water into each bag. Tie up the top of the bag or secure it with a rubber band.

2 Put your bags of water into the freezer. Try squishing and shaping them to create an interesting iceberg shape. Leave the bags overnight to freeze.

3 When the water is frozen, very carefully cut the plastic bags from the two chunks of ice. Fill the large bowl with water.

4 Take one of your icebergs. Observe its shape and draw it in your notebook. Measure and record its height.

5 Now put the iceberg into the bowl. Measure how much of the iceberg is floating above the water's surface.

Compare your two measurements. Is more or less of the iceberg floating under the water?

6 Repeat steps 4 and 5 with your second iceberg.

7 Now ask your adult helper to empty the bowl and fill it with hot water. Ask your helper to carefully put the icebergs into the hot water. Leave them for one hour.

8 Remove the icebergs from the water.

Have your icebergs changed? How? Draw the icebergs and compare your new pictures to the ones you drew earlier.

What do your results tell you about icebergs and warm water?

Glossary

calving
The breaking away of chunks of ice from a glacier or ice sheet. When a chunk of ice calves, it becomes an iceberg.

freshwater
Water that does not contain salt. The water that comes out of faucets is freshwater.

glacier
A giant, thick sheet of ice that very slowly moves downhill like a river of ice.

ice shelf
A huge, floating sheet of ice. An ice shelf forms when a glacier flows down to the sea and keeps going onto the water's surface.

nutrients
Substances, such as iron, that are needed by living things to help them grow and stay healthy.

particles
Tiny pieces of something. For example, soil is made up of tiny particles of rock.

phytoplankton
Tiny, plant-like living things that live in oceans and in freshwater ponds, lakes, and rivers.

thaw
To warm up, melt, and become liquid again.

valley
A low area of land between hills or mountains.

How Do Scientists Name Icebergs?

Scientists at the U.S. National Ice Center track and study very large Antarctic icebergs. When a new giant iceberg is spotted, it's given a name.

The scientists divide Antarctica into four areas—A, B, C, and D. The first part of the iceberg's name shows where it comes from, for example D. Next it is given a number. If the last D area iceberg to be discovered was D-2, the new giant will be called D-3.

If D-3 breaks up, any large pieces will be given a name with their own letter—for example, D-3A, D-3B, D-3C, and so on.

Index

A
animals 20–21
Antarctica 4, 7, 10, 21, 23
Arctic 4

B
B-15 (biggest iceberg) 10–11

C
calving 8, 16
colors of icebergs 16–17, 18

G
glaciers 6–7, 8–9, 16

I
ice shelves 6–7, 8–9, 10

M
melting icebergs 11, 14–15, 18, 20

N
names of icebergs 10–11, 23

S
shapes 14–15, 17, 18, 22
sizes of icebergs 4–5, 9, 10–11, 12–13, 18, 22

Read More

Head, Honor. *Welcome to the Arctic (Nature's Neighborhoods: All About Ecosystems).* Minneapolis, MN: Ruby Tuesday Books (2018).

Lawrence, Ellen. *Say Hello to H_2O (Drip, Drip, Drop: Earth's Water).* Minneapolis, MN: Bearport Publishing (2016).

Answers

Page 9:
Once an iceberg is in the ocean, it gets hit by waves. The Sun may start to melt it, too. Pieces of a large iceberg break away and become smaller icebergs. Sometimes, a large iceberg cracks and breaks into smaller chunks.

Page 15:
The shapes were made by waves crashing against the iceberg. This causes pieces of ice to break away. The water also wears away at the ice.